Black Lake Chronicles

Volume 1

Stories from

The Ottawa Story Spinners

Cathy — Thanks for all your invaluable help with this!

Kit Flynn

Table of Contents

Little Dog Lost, Reiki Found... 1
My Father's Day: The Fateful Phone Call.. 7
William Charles Brain–"OLD NAG"... 11
The Protector... 13
The Day Our House Moved... 17
Secrets, Shysters and Shame.. 23
Apple Peelings and My First Flight.. 29
Buttered Toast, Tea and Stolen Afternoons... 33
St. Anthony Revisited.. 35
The Cliff... 39
Three Dog Tales... 45
Granny's Last Stand at Badminton Road.. 49
The Granny Suite.. 53
Story For Dreyden.. 57
My Path to Happiness.. 59
Rescue at Green Lake.. 69
Tea and Conversation.. 77
Contributors.. 79

Introduction

The Ottawa Story Spinners describes this group perfectly. The group is comprised of eight talented and committed writers with eclectic perceptions about life and the stories within and beyond life. Whether fiction or creative nonfiction, their stories have been woven and spun from a mosaic of life experiences.

The original group was pulled together by Susan Jennings in 2007. Most members at that time were students from writing workshops, with one exception, Barry Alder, who had met Susan at another writers group several years earlier. Unfortunately this first group was abandoned within a year. But with Barry's prodding and encouragement the group started again in the fall of 2008 with two of the original members, Anne Raina and Barry Alder. This time the group quickly grew to eight aspiring writers who have nurtured each others' writing for over two years.

Each member came from a different place but with one goal in mind, to write. Kathi Nidd, happened upon the group through the Ottawa Independent Writers, just as she was thinking of writing a book. Chantal Frobel was looking for something close to home and happened to see an advertisement, recognizing the address as being in her neighbourhood. Kit Flynn was recommended by a mutual colleague through networking; an event Susan only attended once. For Tony and Rita Myres their story of coincidences is quite remarkable. Tony met Susan through the social network on Chapters.ca, subsequently attending a writing workshop together with his wife Rita. Rita and Susan discovered that they were both working on unrelated projects for the same organization, Centrepointe House. The coincidence went one step further as Meghan, Tony and Rita's daughter, had worked with Susan illustrating a book that she was coordinating and editing for Centrepointe House.

Susan firmly believes that no group comes together by accident and it was no accident that brought *The Ottawa Story Spinners* together. As each person joined this writing group it was as though each writer was a vital thread in the weaving of a unique tapestry.

The stories are as eclectic as the authors themselves. The idea of a chapbook was born many months ago with the intention of weaving their stories into a publication. The origin of the term chapbook is intriguing. In the days when pedlars called door to door, selling their goods, they were known as 'chaps'. Among their wares there was often a small book of tales and poems. These books became known as chapbooks. Although, *The Black Lake Chronicles, Volume 1,* at a page count of close to one hundred, is somewhat large for a chapbook, the romantic association of the chapbook origin seems fitting.

The first thread was spun five months ago, but it was at Anne and Grant's cottage, on the shores of Black Lake near Perth, that the group began to weave the idea of a chapbook into reality. The 1st Annual Writer's Retreat took place in August 2010, (illustrated on the front cover). The morning was pleasant as the group sat on the veranda sipping coffee, laughing and talking about writing, and, a rather bizarre subject related to hair styling, which turned into a risqué conversation sending us off into hysterical laughter. Only a group of imaginative writers could weave such tales.

Ask for the story if you dare! Reader discretion is advised!

After feasting on a potluck lunch, the weather began to change. Heavy black clouds rolled over Black Lake and the afternoon brought sheets of torrential rain and howling winds—more fitting for November than August. Oblivious of the weather the group huddled in the cozy living room exchanging stories, many of which would become part of the chapbook.

The howling wind and torrential rain brought more than weather across Black Lake that August day because it was -- that day -- that we realized how special this writer's group had become.

The 2010 Writers Retreat is no doubt the first of many to come.

Thanks to Rita Myres, we now have a name. Subsequent retreats will be known as, *The Ottawa Story Spinner Writers Retreat.*

It is with pride and great pleasure *The Ottawa Story Spinners* presents volume one of The *Black Lake Chronicles.* The Story Spinners will continue to weave their tales into colourful tapestries for many volumes to come.

We hope you will enjoy these eclectic stories and look forward to future volumes.

Written by Susan A Jennings

Acknowledgements

Putting this book together was a collective project. All the authors worked hard, writing their stories, contributing comments and suggestions for both individual stories and decisions about the chapbook. However there are some who have contributed many hours of extra work and deserve a special thank you. Anne Raina, Barry Alder, Tony and Rita Myres for editing; Anne Raina and husband Grant Cameron for their hospitality at Black Lake, as well as their creative photographic staging for the front cover; Barry Alder, for researching and finding a suitable online publisher and for contributing the many hours of manuscript formatting. A very special thank you to Jennifer Alder for her beautiful designs for the front and back cover.

A big thank you to all participants as we could never have pulled this off without your help and commitment to this project.

.

Little Dog Lost, Reiki Found

by Susan A Jennings

The dampness sent a shiver down my spine, as I tied the dogs Buddy and Max-Zee to the tree in the front yard. It was mild for January. Instead of a bone-chilling minus twenty degrees centigrade — typical of Canadian winters in Quebec — the temperature was fluctuating around the freezing point. The heavy snowfalls of December were now coated with a thin crust of ice from the freezing rain. The warmer air temperature had caused a dense mist to hover just above the snow so that bushes and trees appeared to be suspended in an opaque veil. It felt eerie and still. The muffled sounds gave a sense that something unsavory was about to happen.

Trying to escape the January blahs, my friend Kathleen and I were at her brand new house, planning a weekend of pampering ourselves. Curling up in front of a warm fire, Buddy and Max-Zee curled at our feet, watching chick-flicks, and eating popcorn was our escape.

Buddy, a curly white purebred Bichon Frisé, had spent the first three of his five years with Diana and two female Bichon Frisés, Holly and Cricket—Diana was a Buddy Holly fan. He was a breeding dog and had fathered numerous litters. Because of illness, Diana couldn't take care of all three dogs so she was faced with finding a new home for Buddy. Through a series of coincidences I happened on the scene, and Buddy came to live with me.

Max-Zee, Kathleen's dog and Buddy's son, was a wiry, bouncy one-year-old. Buddy's fatherly patience tolerated Max-Zee's antics of pulling his ears and chewing his legs. When it got too much, he would jump on my lap with a pleading look of 'get this kid off me' but never did he snap or growl.

Still in our PJ's at noon, in keeping with our lazy weekend, we were preparing lunch and popping popcorn. The Kleenex strategically placed ready for our tear jerking movie — but that was not to be.

BARK…BARK! Looking out of the window, I could see no strangers or delivery people, only Max-Zee barking. Only Max-Zee! I thought. Where was Buddy? I ran outside but there was no sign of Buddy and his leash was gone. Tears welled up with panic. I ran in the house and pulled jeans over my PJ's, grabbing my coat and boots. My heart was thumping so hard I could hardly breathe. What if I couldn't find him? What if he's been stolen?

"Kathleen!" I yelled, "Buddy has gone!"

Grabbing the car keys I attempted to run, sliding on the ice-covered path, to the car. I stared in disbelief at the ice sculpture that was once my car.

"It will take hours to chip the ice off!" I shouted.

Kathleen had her coat and boots on and called from the front door, "Don't worry about the car. We have a better chance of finding him on foot. Let's each go in a different direction."

I nod okay, but use the remote to start the car anyway, leaving the engine running.

Buddy was a laid-back kind of dog but, with his leash untied, he would just keep walking, with few street smarts, and, in unfamiliar territory, there was no saying where he might end up.

Kathleen's house was surrounded by bush but, for the most part, it was still a construction site. In my panic, I imagined Buddy trapped in a basement, lost in the bush or, my worst fear, headed for the main highway. The panic was taking over as I slipped and slid on the melting ice, darting this way and that. I clambered on snow banks, the crust of ice snapping as I sank to my knees in the soft wet snow, too soft to even hold the weight of a little dog. I panicked again. Could he be stuck in the snow? "Stop!" I said to myself. I must calm down. My eyes strained to see through the shroud of mist. The stillness, eerie and formidable, that unsavory feeling crept down my spine again. My heart sank with every call and every step. I listened...but there was only muffled silence. I was consumed with fear.

I heard my inner voice whisper, "Reiki...Reiki, let the Universe guide you," I chastised myself. As a Reiki Master I should have thought of it sooner. The natural positive energy of Reiki was just what I needed to calm my fear-mongering brain chatter. I took a deep breath, closed my eyes and asked for guidance.

The fear abated and, my head clearer, I knew I must fetch the car. I was relieved to see the warmth from the engine had shed the capsule of sculptured ice. I set out—I don't know where. I drove down one street calling, calling and up another calling again, but there was no sign of Buddy. My intuition told me he was not far away.

I said aloud, "Buddy, be safe and stay where you are, I will find you."

Now I was focused enough to plan my search. The plan would take me down each street until I reached the main road. At this point if I turned left I could cover the whole neighbourhood. The plan went well until the anticipated left turn. The street was blocked with barricades, and my heart sank—now what? The barricade forced me to turn right onto a busy road, which was definitely not in my plan. I tried to stay calm while looking for a turning lane, but there was nowhere to turn. I drove slowly but the traffic behind me was impatient... HONK! HONK! I sped up only to slow down for the approaching traffic lights. Thank goodness! Now I could turn. Thwarted again, as I stopped for the red light I saw the sign...NO LEFT TURNS. This was too much. My eyes burning with tears and my confidence shot, for a second time I was forced to turn right. The road was narrow with tall hedges on each side, I felt claustrophobic. Where was I? Fearful that I would get lost, tears of despair sat on my eyelids. The car laboured up a steep incline. I was jerked back to reality as a truck appeared on the crest of the hill. My heart missed a beat as I quickly pulled over and we passed with barely an inch to spare.

At the top of the hill it was brighter; a weak sun was struggling through the veil of mist. I could see a children's playground and open bush-land. My spirits rose as it looked familiar. I realized I was looking at the same bush that ran alongside Kathleen's house. I scanned the horizon for movement, and there was only stillness... but wait...I thought I heard something. I leaned my head out of the car window and my senses picked up a slight whimper. My eyes drifted downwards and there he was, sitting patiently, waiting, his trusting brown eyes fixed on me with his head cutely to one side, his leash still attached. My heart filled with joy and gratitude as I drove carefully towards him. He didn't move. I parked the car and he still didn't move. I smiled, remembering my own words, "Buddy, be safe and stay where you are, I will find you." He had listened.

"Come, Buddy, come!" I called and he leapt into my arms, licks and doggy kisses (which are not normally allowed) all over my face; his head nestled in my shoulder. I could feel his little heart beating a mile a minute. The tears, now uncontrollable, tumbled down my face as I hugged my precious Buddy.

Wet, cold and tired, we drove back to find Kathleen and Max-Zee anxiously waiting. After much hugging and tears—the Kleenex, put to good use long before the movie, we settled down. Buddy snuggled tightly at my side, all of us sitting just a little closer, appreciating the warmth of the fire and the safety of home.

I believe it was the power of Reiki's universal energy that told Buddy to sit and wait and that same energy calmed, comforted and guided me to the playground, making sure I could not turn. If I had been able to stick to my plan, I would have been miles away from Buddy and, if I had kept searching on foot, I would never have found him. There was definitely something more than misty, freezing rain in the air that cold, damp January day. Reiki guided and protected both of us, bringing the search for Buddy to a safe and happy ending.

What is Reiki?

Reiki is an ancient Japanese technique discovered by Dr Mikao Usui in the early 1900s. Rei – means universal in that, energy is all around us and part of us. Some interpret this as spiritual wisdom coming from a higher place. Ki – means the same as Chi in Chinese, life – energy, which is a non-physical energy living in all things. Reiki energy helps the body, mind and spirit to heal a multitude of ailments and conditions. It is an all knowing universal energy that is limitless and can do no harm. Trusting, believing and practicing Reiki, either formally or informally, not only benefits the individual but all living things.

Dogs, in fact all animals, are particularly receptive to Reiki energy. They are instinctive, live close to nature and have no human inhibitions or beliefs. Reiki energy is used effectively to treat dogs with separation anxiety, soothe the pain of arthritis and much more.

Reiki practitioners/teachers undergo stringent training and are attuned to act as a conduit for the flow of Reiki energy.

Susan A. Jennings RMT, IARP
Registered Reiki Professional

My Father's Day: The Fateful Phone Call

by Tony Myres

It was Friday, October 30th, 1992, when my 16 year old son, Graham, handed me a piece of paper on which was written my Father's name, Herbert Angelo Myres, and a telephone number in Lake Charles, Louisiana. Could this really be him? My dad - words I'd never spoken in 48 years. I ruminated over this question all weekend, conjuring up many different scenarios. What if it all was a mistake? Suppose it was him and he denied me, rejected me a second time? What would my mother, quietly living upstairs in our house, as she had for the past 15 years since emigrating to Canada, think of all this? I was scared. I didn't know what to do. I prayed a lot that weekend. When I awoke on Monday morning, I knew I had to pick up the phone and dial that number. Even then, having made the decision, I did not do it straight away. I set myself a time to do it in the afternoon. Then I pushed it back an hour. Never had the telephone seemed daunting. At 2:00 PM., I picked up the phone with sweaty hands and thumping heart, and dialed the number.

As I dialed and listened to the ringing tones, my mind carried me back to when I was a little boy and had asked "Where is my dad?", and was always told by my gran with whom I lived with my mum, "He didn't come back from the war." Probably a good enough reason for a little boy who had many friends whose fathers hadn't come back because they were killed. Eventually, in my early teens, I learned the truth. I was an abandoned war baby.

I was struck out of my reverie by an old man's voice at the other end of the line. Well, this is it, I thought as I began my carefully prepared script which I had run over in my mind so many times. "Hello, is that Herbert Angelo Myres?"

"Yeah" came a rather suspicious reply.

"My name is Tony Myres from Canada. I know this is a bit of a long shot, but were you, by any chance, in the US Army and stationed in Bristol, England during the Second World War?"

"Yeah," came the even more suspicious response.

There were shock waves going through me at this point as I grasped the phone so hard I thought I was going to break it, and blurted out, "Well," my throat constricting as I said it, "That means you must be my dad!"

There was a silence that seemed to go on forever and then a soft voice in a deep southern accent, "Well, I rekun tha's rite - yu mus' be mah boy!"

We were both so stunned by the discovery of each other that there was a silence. Then he said how sorry he was for what happened.

"I had nothin' heah for yus both. I thought yor momma and you be better off with yor granny. She'd look after you better'n I could. Make sure you'd have an edicashun an that."

There was a pause, "I neva forgot yu'all - I still got the baby picture of ya." At this point we were so overcome that we lapsed into a conversation of short factual questions and answers.

Yes, my mum was still alive and now living with me in Canada. No, she had never remarried. Neither had he and I remember feeling a pang of disappointment that I hadn't discovered some half brothers and sisters. I told him that he had three grandchildren. He said softly, "Yeah - ain't that sweet."

Before we hung up, I said I would write to him that night and enclose pictures of his "new" family and I would fly down to see him as soon as I could

The next evening the phone rang and it was dad. "I had to call ya. I jus' wanna be sure it's true. Cos' if it ain't, I think I'm gonna' die."

I assured him it was indeed true, the letter and pictures were in the mail and I had purchased my air ticket and would be down to see him within two weeks.

On my trip I took with me lots of photos, both old and new, including pictures of his wedding to my mum and various memorabilia of my own life. How difficult it was to contain almost 50 years of life into a set of photographs and pieces of paper. I took copies of my university degrees and even my school reports, for these were things in which there would have been a shared joy and pride had he been there at the time.

On that first trip, I showed dad a photo of our old house in Bristol where my mum had spent her entire life until coming to Canada in 1978.

"Do you remember the house?, I asked.

"Yeah - I 'member that house aw'right." There was a long passage with them doors on each side. I ony eva went in that back room where yor granny and yor momma was."

Did he remember grandfather? "I hardly eva seen him - he wus always down at that shop o' his. S'ony yor momma an' granny I can 'member now."

I have sometimes thought back to that day, painting in my mind again, as I did before phoning, various "what if" scenarios. All of them were theoretical because the reality is that I did find the courage to pick up the phone and make the call and find the true answer to the question "Whatever happened to my Dad?"

That day I phoned will always be known to me as 'My Father's Day'!

William Charles Brain–"OLD NAG"

by Tony Myres

W.C. Brain was born in Bristol in 1880 into a fairly well established west country family whose roots go back to the time of William the Conqueror. W.C. married Maud Dicker on Christmas Day, 1901 and they had three children; Albert(1902), Beatrice(1908), and Norma(1924), my mother, who gave birth to me in 1944.

I remember my grandfather was a rather mysterious, shadowy, frowned upon figure in our home at 37 Badminton Road in Bristol. He had his own rooms, his meals were taken separately (I was often the waiter!), spent every day down at a mysterious place called "the shop", and was, generally speaking, a miserable cantankerous, complaining old man given, as my grandmother used to say "to fits of bawling and shouting". Not surprisingly he was known in my family as Old Nag and, as a very young child, for a long time I thought this was his real name until the occasional but unusual reference to "our dad" by my mother gave the game away and I realized he was my grandfather. He was a bakery engineer by profession and was quite successful at it until the late 1920s when he started down the hill to financial ruin — he became an inveterate gambler. I well remember the often heard phrase "he's pickin 'em out" meaning, of course, he was studying the form of horses and dogs. Unfortunately he did not pick many winners...the money ran out, the bakery engineering business failed and he bought a shop. The shop, originally intended for antiques, like most of his ventures was not a success and became a junk shop. Old Nag would have sold anything, so my grandmother started to lock things up at home. She had a bunch of keys which never left her person. This may seem an extreme measure but one day he did take up the stair carpet and sold it! He died in 1954 when I was 10 and all that was left for his wife and three children was the princely sum of nineteen pounds (approx $40) each. The four grandchildren came off best because we were left fifty pounds to be held in trust until we reached the age of 21. This milestone for me was reached in 1965. It was a timely windfall for me for shortly after I became engaged to Rita and so with my "loot" I was able to buy her an engagement ring and begin a loving relationship that has lasted for over 40 years.

The Protector

by Kathi Nidd

Moonlight illuminated my living room through the large picture window. I could not help but look outside. It had snowed again overnight but now the sky was a clear February blue. Random speckles sparkled as if someone had sewn sequins on the white cover that was my front lawn. I welcomed the silence of the night. I could hear the low motor of the fridge and the gentle dripping of a distant tap. These sounds, always present, were usually silenced by daytime commotion. I stood watching each of my neighbours' houses, cozy and safe and free from the brightness and turmoil of the day.

Insomnia was becoming more of a rule than an exception. In the past few months the strain of grief and stress had bore holes into my sleep like a jackhammer. Nights were no longer a fluid, linear period of time, but instead short segments of peace divided by jagged blocks of nightmares and worry. I was struggling to move past the stages of grief following the tragic loss of my dear friend, Hal.

I stared at the snow and suddenly noticed a rabbit before me on the lawn. I had not seen it hop by nor were there any paw prints in the snow between the driveway and where it stood. It was small, brown and white and, although facing me directly, it was not really looking at me. Its nose twitched as it peered about. I willed it to look directly at me but, of course, the rabbit was busy, watching for predators and listening for any noise that could indicate danger.

I felt blessed that I had woken up early and got to bear witness to this beautiful creature. Likely he sat on my front lawn every night while I was in bed unaware. I glanced behind me at the clock, 3:11, and then turned back to the window. The rabbit had vanished, again without a trace of prints in the soft snow.

Hal would have loved seeing this. He loved wildlife and would have been intrigued by the apparent lack of footprints. In fact, Hal would have said the rabbit was a sign. An avid believer in the afterlife, Hal always saw nature as significant demonstrations and signals from beyond. He even used to joke with me that if he were to pass away first, he would contact me from beyond and, on some level, I believed him.

We had grown up as next door neighbours. I cannot remember a moment that he was not part of my life in my fifty years. Childhood playmates, then teenage pals, Hal and I had gone through every stage of life as one, even attending the same college where he'd become a journalist and I a lawyer. Despite the obvious coaxes from our parents and friends, Hal and I had never become a couple nor felt any romance. We were just family. As we'd grown up and had families of our own, our spouses had also become friends.

But, two months had passed since the first ice storm had forced the courier truck to skid out of control on Spruce Street and slam into the driver's door of Hal's Mazda. No magical forces from Hal had contacted me from beyond. Part of me was happy; for the so-called "experts" explained that it meant he had crossed over peacefully. But part of me was hoping for some contact. After all, losing loved ones did cause one to search for the comfort in believing that those lost were still alive in some way.

I melted into our puffy Lazy Boy chair as I felt my eyes grow heavy. As I let my mind wander, I recalled Hal's favourite ghost story.

He had been house-sitting, he'd told me, several years ago for a friend who lived in the country just outside of Ottawa. Hal had promised to drop by the old farmhouse every few days to make sure the pipes hadn't frozen while his friend vacationed in Mexico. On his second trip to the house, he had arrived at dusk, let himself in, and walked from room to room making sure everything remained intact. As he walked, he swore he had heard footsteps behind him and, at one point, he had even pivoted quickly to try to catch what was making the noise behind him. Feeling uneasy and somewhat silly, he poured himself a scotch and seated himself at the large wooden kitchen table. He tried to convince himself it was just the creaks and rattles of the old house playing tricks on his tired mind. To calm his nerves, he picked up one of last week's newspapers from the pile on the table and attempted to focus on an article. Suddenly, outside the large picture window behind him, something caught his eye. A large buck stood, staring into the kitchen and down the hall. Hal watched while the animal stood perfectly still, its head bowed knowingly.

After a few minutes, he recounted, he heard the footsteps again. Willing the source of the noise to go away, he tried to keep his eyes fixated on the newspaper. But soon curiosity won. Gradually, reluctantly, he lifted his eyes from the paper. A young girl of about seven or eight lingered a few feet away. She had long, curly blond hair and was wearing a long red dress with a white lace collar. At the bottom of her dress, he noticed, her legs were missing. Yet as he watched she seemingly skipped along the hallway, her head rising and falling with each impossible step. He turned away from the girl and back towards the window. The buck, who had been staring the whole time, lifted its front paws and darted off into the woods. When he turned back, the little girl had vanished.

Hal shared the experience with his wife, who agreed to return with him the next morning to check on the house again. That morning and all subsequent visits, the house was empty. He never saw the little girl again and the homeowner, who had never seen or heard anything like it, never reported anything similar. Hal shared his story with me many times as he tirelessly tried to justify it.

Now, sitting in the dead quiet of night, I replayed the story again and smiled. I was always enthralled by Hal's story telling. Silently, I willed him to contact me, as I gradually fell into a peaceful sleep.

The following afternoon, with apprehension, I turned my car onto Spruce Street and began heading westward. In the two months following Hal's accident, I had done everything I could to avoid the intersection that had taken his life. A known high risk corner, the local authorities had begun a campaign to look into why the corner was so terrible. The area was mostly country and surrounded by bush, but recent subdivisions had led to increased traffic that hadn't been well predicted by planners. Usually I could avoid it by taking another route, but this afternoon I was running desperately late for an appointment with a client and it seemed the only logical choice.

I glanced at the clock on the dashboard, 3:11. My appointment was at 3:15 and there was no way I would make it. I decided to pull over and call to let them know I was running late. I pulled out of traffic to the dirt shoulder and stopped the car next to a patch of brush to call my client and explain that I would be late. As I hung up, I started the car again and was about to merge back into traffic when I was overcome with the feeling that someone was watching me. There, standing, no more than three feet in front of me, a buck stood like a statue. Without fear, it calmly watched me. Mesmerized, and reminded of Hal's story, I stayed parked for several minutes.

Then I heard the screech, the shrill sound of metal and pavement, the penetrating crash as the minivan catapulted forward beside me and slammed into the car in front. In seeming slow motion, I watched as one by one the cars piled up into a horizontal stack at the spot where my car would have been. I sat parallel to them in the safety of the shoulder and watched the buck dart away in fear from the noise.

The next morning the local paper reported on the accident. An eight year old girl, Ashley Donovan, had passed away after having her legs crushed by the van that had rear ended her mother's car. A colour picture of Ashley, beside the article, displayed blond curls cascading down her shoulders onto her red dress and white lace collar.

The Day Our House Moved

By Anne Raina

What forces of nature could cause a house to move? An earthquake? Gale-force winds? A mud slide? Or, a man named Mr. Carlisle?

When a house moves, it does not always fall off its crumbling foundation. Sometimes it moves on to a solid foundation! That's what my home did when I was seven years old.

The youngest of ten children, I grew up on a farm three miles south of Kemptville, Ontario, which is thirty miles south of Ottawa. Our farmhouse was located one quarter of a mile from Old Highway 16, or the King's Highway, as it was sometimes called. Our home lay at the end of a long grassy lane, bordered on both sides for the first half by huge, towering, thick cedar trees, which were really part of the bush that encroached upon our access. At the halfway point, the lane turned slightly to the right, like a barely bent elbow. From that spot we emerged into open pasture on either side and there, at the end of the lane, stood our home, always so welcoming to everyone.

Being so far removed from the highway meant we had no access to hydro, which, in turn, meant we had no access to indoor plumbing. Early each morning my mother would polish the smoke-smudged globes of our coal oil lamps and our beautiful Aladdin lamp. She would use old newspaper to make those globes fairly sparkle. At no time, to my knowledge, as she rubbed the Aladdin lamp, did a genie ever appear. I'm quite sure we would have been told, if such an event had occurred. Mom would refill the oil and turn up the wick and have the lamps all lined up and ready for evening time.

As darkness fell, a match would be taken from the tin matchbox holder mounted on our kitchen wall. A box of wooden matches just fit into the holder and, with a rapid wrist motion, the match scratched along the holder would ignite into a blue flame. The smell of sulfur would linger as the lamps were lit. Magically, they would cast their light on the table where my siblings and I played games or did homework, or rolled bits of mercury around to break into little globules and then join them together again in one big, silvery blob. The subdued lighting would barely extend to the chair and desk where my Father did his books and valiantly stretched to reach the loveseat where my mother sat darning socks or sewing buttons on our shirts or blouses. These lamps always brought a welcome coziness and reassuring warmth to the room.

    As for not having indoor plumbing, I always thought our outhouse far outclassed those of my country friends. We had a lovely glass window which let the sunlight stream in during the day and the moonlight at night. Mom also papered the inside of our outdoor privy with the large pieces of wallpaper samples that we would receive each spring time. There were so many patterns that it was always a pleasant experience just deciding on each visit which flowers or stripes looked prettiest on a particular day. It was located in an area in which our cows pastured. For the most part, it was a friendly outhouse, as outhouses go, except for one memorable exception. One day, when I was four years old, I was sitting there innocently admiring, once again, Mom's lovely decorating scheme. Suddenly, everything went pitch black. Startled and frightened I looked at the window. The window was completely blacked out and, by the sliver of light filtering through the door frame, I was able to barely discern two ENORMOUS brown eyes staring at me through the window. I let out a blood curdling scream. Quickly, but not fast enough to suit me, my brother Nick came running to the door to rescue me. Nick had, from the vantage point of the window in our dining room, seen a cow headed straight for the outhouse and knew what was going to happen next. He had gathered our siblings to listen to the scream that they knew was going to follow as the cow stuck her face directly into the window frame. They were not disappointed!

    All of us loved living back in, what would now likely be considered, the wilderness. But the lane to the highway was long. Many of my siblings had tuberculosis and were in the hospital in Ottawa. Others were reaching the age when they were leaving home to seek job opportunities elsewhere. And my Father, terminally ill with tuberculosis, was soon coming home from the hospital to die. It was obvious that my Mother and the younger children should not be left to face winters in such total isolation. What was the solution then, to this impending dilemma? We certainly couldn't move the hydro lines and highway closer to us. There was only one logical answer. We would move our house to the highway and hydro lines.

With that decision made, it was time to formulate a plan. In the spring of 1951, Mr. Carlisle was contacted and contracted. Our house had to be jacked up and the gigantic moving float positioned carefully into place underneath it. We only had a dirt cellar and now we had to climb higher steps to get into our home as it was elevated into position for the move. Some of the men attending to the preparations ate meals with us frequently, while they worked to ready everything. I was fascinated when, at the end of the meal, one of them would take a little round tin box out of the pocket of his overalls and remove a pinch of some dark brown looking stuff that reminded me a bit of ground up pencil shavings or crumpled dried hay. It looked to be in little stringy bits. He would then shove this under his upper lip. I found this ritual mesmerizing and, if I had known the word then, exceedingly gross. In spite of his penchant for using snuff, he was a very nice man.

Watching the preparations for the move of the house held me captivated. I would look on from my vantage point beneath the two huge apple trees right beside our home and occasionally I felt pangs about leaving them. I loved those trees. We had many family meals in their shade. Often on Sundays, when we returned from Mass, Mom would spread the tablecloth under the trees and serve platters of her delicious fried chicken, new potatoes and vegetables from the garden and haul out trays laden with Golden Bantam corn on the cob, tender and dripping with newly churned butter. Mom's fresh bread and her homemade pies were always irresistible treats. Under these same trees we shared so much laughter, conversation and thinking time. One of them was always home base when we played hide and seek. And my brothers and I loved eating the little green sour apples when they were no bigger than large marbles, dousing them with salt. On Holy Saturday afternoons, after we children had cleaned the yard in preparation for Easter, we often found that the Easter Bunny had paid an advance short visit and scattered a few small, brightly-wrapped, chocolate eggs under these trees to let us know that he would be arriving again during the night.

There was a big natural sand pile to play in back here, and a hill to slide down. A long, wide row of purple lilac bushes grew close to our home and stretched down through the field. In May, their vibrant purple colour was in startling contrast to the greenery surrounding them, and their fragrance filled the air as soon as one turned the bend in the lane.

The house, when it moved, would be leaving behind our barn. There was more than the usual connection between these two buildings. Years before, one of the previous owners of our farm had met a tragic death here. One day, in haying season, he had been riding atop a load of hay that was being taken into the barn. The horses bolted and the man struck the beam at the top of the large barn door. His neck was broken and he was brought into the house, where he died a few days later.

While the preparatory changes were going on here at home, things were happening at the other end of our lane. Well, not exactly at the other end. About three quarters of the way down our lane towards the highway, the land, quite rocky and with a stone base there, took a noticeable slope downwards to the right, between the trees. It would be down that section that the house would be moved. When it reached the bottom of the hill, the moving float would turn to the left and deposit our home on to the new foundation being built there, in a clearing. My brothers and I frequently explored the new basement area for our house. Having a basement with a floor in it and stairs to reach it would be quite the novelty for all of us.

A short distance down the highway was a newly-opened little restaurant and store and, very occasionally, because spending money was scarce, we would walk down there on hot days and purchase an orange crush. We would return to the area of the rising foundation, sit down beside it, and slowly sip the tangy orange liquid from the bottle made of dark brown, thick and ridged glass, bearing the Orange Crush label. What a treat. We would each be lost in our own thoughts of what this move would mean.

The day finally arrived when all was in readiness. I left for school in the morning and, as usual, walked down the long lane to catch the school bus. The air was pungent with the smell of cedar and, also as usual, I kept a wary eye over my shoulder to see if the cows were following me. One of them was quite aggressive and I never liked to see her appear around the bend in the lane. It was always a relief to climb between the bars of the gate that separated the end of our lane from the highway.

I had often found it a relief to climb through those bars for another reason. On rainy days, when I had to walk under the hydro lines, I always feared that somehow I could get an electric shock from the raindrops dripping from those lines. Someone had warned me of that danger and it was a warning I heeded. When it rained I ran as fast as I could under those lines, praying that somehow the electrically-charged drops would miss me. Miraculously, they always did!

Soon I climbed on to the school bus and set off for another routine day in class. This day was really not quite as routine though, as throughout the day I found myself distracted by trying to picture how a house could actually move. That day seemed to crawl by and I couldn't wait to get home. My excitement and curiosity mounted as the school bus got closer and closer to home. I wished the children would get off the bus quicker at their stops. They seemed to be moving in slow motion. And the bus driver seemed to be driving so slowly. Finally, my stop came into view. But something else came into view as well. My home was sitting in the clearing, mature cedars, pines and tamarack trees offering their protection to this new, but really old, home, just moved into their landscape. Our familiar house was now perched atop its new foundation, just as welcoming as it had always been. Except that now, I did not have to walk down a long lane to reach it.

I stopped for a minute and looked at it. When I left for school that morning my home was way back, surrounded by fields. When I got off the school bus just now, my home was right here, close to the highway, hydro poles nearby and traffic buzzing by, going fast.

I ran into the house as quickly as I could for my welcome hug from Mom and to ask about the move. Mom excitedly told me she had not even had to put out the fire in the wood stove during the move. She described how the smoke had wafted out the chimney as the house moved along on its journey. No jostling. No mishaps. Not a dish had cracked and there had been no damage, not even coming down that steep slope. And our home fit perfectly on its new foundation. We all considered the events of this day quite an astonishing feat. Now, when we looked out our front windows, instead of seeing fields and trees, we saw lawn and highway, with bush filling in our vision beyond the pavement.

From that day, ever after, the location from where our home had been moved has always been referred to as 'the old place'.

Soon we would have electricity. We were spellbound as holes were drilled here and there in the ceilings and walls and black electrical wire was shoved into those crevices and disappeared to snake, goodness knew where, throughout the house. At five dollars an outlet for installation costs, this addition to our home was expensive, but deemed necessary. What a transformation that was. You pulled a chain and the light came on. Imagine! Next we acquired a real refrigerator. No longer did we lower perishables in a bucket into our well to keep them cold and we now had no need for the ice man to deliver blocks of ice for our small, brown, wooden ice box.

We got new siding on our house, and, in a few years, indoor plumbing would follow. There were many changes, most of them good, and some that we knew would not be good.

We would never have two apple trees beside our home again. We would not have my Father either. He died shortly after I turned eight years old. But a little pine tree was planted to the left of our home before my Father died. It grew as I grew and provided me always with strong, loving memories of my Father. Today that tree is fifty-nine years old. It stands tall, stately and can be seen from a very long distance. It has many children of its own!

It always reminds me of the day our house moved.

Secrets, Shysters and Shame

By Susan A. Jennings

The clickety clack rhythm of the train lulled Marci into a half sleep, enabling her to relax and think. She frowned as she recalled her friend's unusually shrill voice and the defiant click as the phone went dead; it was so unlike Judy. The pit of her stomach was telling her something was very wrong and that was why she was heading to Toronto uninvited. Deep in thought, Marci's furrowed brow relaxed into a smile as she remembered their first meeting at M & F Foods. They were so different. Judy's petite doll like figure, adorned in pink frills, contrasted Marci's tall slender frame, dressed in a tailored pant suit. A casualty of the recession, Judy had been laid off a few years later. Marci, protected by seniority, stayed until she retired. Even living in different cities hadn't hindered their friendship.

The train slowly came to a stop, and Marci caught a cab directly to Judy's place. Judy was sitting on the porch surrounded by flowers, and framed by the bay window and its pretty lace curtains. So in character, Marci thought affectionately.

"Surprise!" Marci said, hoping she sounded more confident than she felt.

"I had a feeling you wouldn't take no for an answer," Judy said, standing on tip toes and hugging Marci, "You look good."

"So do you," Marci lied. Black circles rimmed Judy's eyes. Her smile had lost its impish sparkle. The pale blue jacket hung limply from her shoulders. Marci knew she had done the right thing by coming.

The phone was ringing but Judy ignored it. "Telemarketers," she said. As soon as the ringing stopped it started again. This time Judy answered.

"Are you threatening me?" Judy whispered. "No wait... I'll see what I can do."

"What was that all about?" Marci inquired

"Umm... nothing. I'll make tea. Could you grab the milk?"

Marci opened the fridge. "Oh my goodness! There's nothing in here."

"I wasn't expecting guests, remember?" They both laughed. "We'll go shopping tomorrow."

The next morning, just as they were driving away, a man walked up to the front door but Judy kept going.

"Someone is at your door," Marci said, "and he looks kind of sleazy."

"Oh... that's the hydro guy."

They shopped all day, arriving home exhausted. Marci started to unload the parcels and suddenly pointed across the street, "Look! Isn't that the hydro guy?"

Judy stopped dead, her colour drained to a ghostly white and she was gasping for breath. Marci ran to her, afraid she was having a fit or stroke.

"Judy, what's wrong?"

"I'm okay," Judy huffed. "I know it is...uh... Thursday ...uh... and I can talk... I am not having a stroke." She tried to laugh.

Still worried, Marci sorted the parcels, placed a bag of groceries on the counter and carried the rest upstairs. The phone rang again.

Marci crept to the top of the stairs to listen.

"Please... I can only give you two hundred."

Marci went cold. Was Judy being blackmailed?

"Marci! I'm just popping next door. I forgot the milk."

That's strange. I'm sure we bought some, thought Marci, stepping over to the window. She watched Judy walk directly to the sleazy hydro guy's car and hand him an envelope. The man was angry and shook his fist yelling, "I want the rest tomorrow!"

Judy turned around, her face wet with tears. Marci leapt downstairs and out the door.

"Why are you being blackmailed?"

"Blackmailed!"

"Please, Judy, don't shut me out."

"I'm broke!"

"Broke!" Marci repeated, "So you are being blackmailed."

"Why do you keep talking about blackmail?"

"Well, let's see. The phone calls, the stake-out, the sleazy hydro guy, a suspicious envelope; not to mention how upset you are. Need I say more?" Marci was frustrated. "I can see it with my own eyes."

"Oh my goodness... Marci...he's a bill collector!" Half laughing, half crying, Judy explained, "I'm afraid to answer the phone; I'm spied on, threatened and constantly harassed. I am scared to leave the house." She busied herself at the kitchen counter.

Marci put two and two together. Judy's strange behaviour, why there was no food in the fridge. All of today's shopping was hers except for one small bag of groceries. She felt guilty. She did have a pension and savings and had assumed Judy did too. How could she have been so blind?

Judy placed two steaming mugs on the table and they fell silent, sipping the comforting tea. Judy stared pensively as she talked about the slippery slope from middle class affluence to the fast approaching 'bag lady' poverty.

"After I was laid off, I never found a good job with benefits. Every month I supplemented with my savings until they were gone. Now I rely on the government pension, which doesn't even cover basic expenses." Judy stared into her tea. "I did something very foolish. I borrowed money from one of those money places."

Marci was shocked. "Those guys are all shysters! Why didn't you tell me?"

"Well, at first they seemed really nice and helpful. I thought I could handle it. I planned to sell the car and pay them back but the car didn't sell. I couldn't make the payments and they became very nasty. I thought of selling the house but where would I go? " Judy gave a nervous giggle. "Sleazy hydro guy thinks that I'm a spoiled middle-class housewife hiding some unforgivable monetary sin from my husband." They started laughing hysterically at the irony of this, as they were both long time divorcees.

Marci took advantage of the mood change to take control of the situation.

"As I see it, the first thing we do tomorrow morning is pay off these shysters."

Judy protested, "I can't --"

"This is not negotiable," Marci said forcefully. "I have the money, consider it a loan. After that, we'll pick up groceries and a bottle of wine."

The following evening they shared the wine and brainstormed

ideas until they were satisfied they had a realistic plan that would meet Judy's needs. Pleased with the results, Marci raised her glass.

"To prosperity and no more secrets!"

The glasses gave a TING as they touched.

"To prosperity and no more secrets!"

Marci smiled as she saw the impish sparkle back in Judy's smile.

Apple Peelings and My First Flight

By Anne Raina

The last Monday of August 1949 was a desperately hot day. I was 5 years old and, although I was the youngest of 10 children, I was feeling, as I sometimes did, very lonely. My next sibling, Jim, was almost six years older than me and he, with some of my other brothers, was doing farm chores. Our farmhouse was some distance from the highway and far removed from any children my age with whom I could play. In fact, I rarely got to play with anyone close to my age. And I had outgrown my make-believe friends Mabbel (as in babble, not Mabel as in table) and the other girl to whom I never did give a name. Sometimes Mabbel and I didn't like her too much. There was nothing about the way the day started that would have foretold that I would be taking a most unusual trip before the day was over.

Mom was always a ready and eager listener when I wanted to chatter with her and her lap was available anytime I wanted to crawl up for a cherished, loving hug. But that day the house was so hot that by afternoon I didn't want to be indoors. I didn't know how my Mother could stand to stay anywhere near the heat blasting out from our wood stove in our kitchen. We had no electricity and no running water and it was stifling indoors. I hated that kind of oppressive heat - it always made me feel sick and lethargic.

Earlier that morning there had still been a bit of a breeze when Mom heated the water for a big washing she was doing. Up and down her hands and arms flew as she erased, like magic, the grime and dirt from the men's work clothes on the scrub board she maneuvered with amazing dexterity. Of course, she had done this many times before!

Then the various items got tossed into the tub of the old wringer washer for a good rinse before being fed through the wringer.

Sometimes I got to turn the crank. I really enjoyed other times when Mom let me put the smaller items of clothing through the wringer, judging when one item had disappeared to the point where it was time to feed in the next piece. A little overlapping was alright. My Mother watched me carefully as she turned the wringer crank. Often I would ask her to tell me again the story of the little girl whose mother was distracted while she turned the wringer and the little girl's hand and then her arm went through the wringer right up to her shoulder. Mom had grown up out west and this had happened to a neighbour's child and Mom said the little girl could never use her arm properly again. This story guaranteed that I would be very careful where my fingers were as I fed the numerous items through the little girl, arm-eating rollers.

    I eagerly awaited the go-ahead from my Mother to unwrap a small square of bluing and then watched the water turn inky blue when my Mother gave me permission to add it to the rinse water. It seemed to me that it would be impossible for the linens and our white clothes to be any brighter or whiter than my Mother got them in the wash. But then, once the clothesline was full, she laid our sheets and pillow cases on the grass and low bushes to dry. When those were brought in they fairly sparkled and smelled fresher and cleaner than the outdoors itself.

    However, following the washing there was always a huge ironing to be done. My Mother would stand by the ironing board, in that hot kitchen, beads of perspiration running down her face and dripping on to the ironing board. Back and forth she would go to the stove. She would place the cooling iron she was using back in its holder on the stove to reheat and pick up the hot one waiting. Back at the ironing board, she would touch her mouth with her forefinger and quickly touch the bottom of the iron. She knew from the sizzle of the spittle if the iron was hot enough to get the creases out but not so hot that it would scorch the spotless clothes. Most of the clothes had already been sprinkled to help them iron up totally crease-free. My Mother was so quick in these movements. An article of laundry would be laid out on the table. Close at hand was a blue, speckled tin bowl holding water. Quick as a flash Mom would dip her fingers into the water in the bowl and sprinkle the item of clothing. She would immediately roll it up so it would retain its dampness until it was time for the iron to do its work, guided by my Mother. And then there were the items that needed starching. In a large washbasin Mom would make a pasty mixture and dip the doilies, white shirts, blouses or tablecloths into the solution. Then they would be wrung out and ironed within an inch of their lives for my Mother was not one to let wrinkles survive if she could help it.

On this day, by the time I had watched my Mother iron for a while, I couldn't take the heat anymore. I didn't yet know the expression 'if you can't stand the heat get out of the kitchen' but that's what I did. Outside did not provide much of a relief.

It was so hot it was a buzzing day. In the house there had been the zzzzzing of black flies stuck to the yellow fly hangers, hanging in the far corner of the kitchen, its sticky coating lying in wait to trap the silly, unwary flies. Outside there was the buzz of grasshoppers hopping everywhere in the dry grass, their knees clicking. And, not far off, the hottest buzzing sound of all - the rising and falling drone of the cicada, a sound that just permeates your head with the feeling of hot and muggy.

I wandered around our big yard, lay down on my back for a while and watched the lazy clouds floating overhead. Even the sheep, car, haystack and big spoon I saw up there looked hot. After sitting for a time in the shade of the apple trees beside our house, I went down our lane and picked a bouquet of wildflowers and proudly presented them to Mom. She welcomed me with a hug and a kiss and the Brown-eyed Susans, buttercups and pink clover with delight and put them in a glass which she placed in the centre of our table. She told me they would pretty up our supper that night.

The ironing board had been put away and now there was a tantalizing aroma of apple pies baking. There could not be fresher apple pies. Mom had just picked the apples and peeled and cored and tucked them into her scrumptious pastry and popped the pie plates into the oven to be ready in time for our meal.

After I had set the table for supper and, as I headed out the kitchen door on more ramblings, Mom asked me to take the basket heaped with apple peelings and dump them for the cows that by now were impatiently waiting in the barnyard to be taken in to be milked. Even they looked hot, swishing their tails to keep the flies away and wearing vacant expressions as they slowly and methodically chewed their cuds. I skipped over to the gate and crawled between the rungs and in with the cows. A white cow, Daisy, was my favourite so I wanted her to have first chance at this special treat. I walked in front of her and upturned the basket of peelings.

Just then our collie, Towser, raced in between me and Daisy and started barking ferociously at her. He was between the cow and the peelings at my feet. Daisy, usually so good natured, resented this interference with the treat awaiting her. Faster than I had ever seen her move before, she lowered her head and charged at the barking dog. Towser, like any clever dog would, speedily got out of the way of those horns but the cow, not having a good braking system, kept coming. Before I knew what had happened I was sailing through the air and over the fence. Kerthump! I landed in a heap of arms and legs on the lap of my 17 year-old brother George who was sitting on top of a pile of rocks, with his back to the barnyard. Completely oblivious to the drama unfolding behind his back, he was totally shocked to have this flying object descend on him so abruptly. I was stunned to be there. There was little doubt that if George had not been sitting there I would likely have been seriously hurt. And I don't think it was my imagination that Towser looked concerned when he trotted over to watch me disentangle myself. To this day I have no idea where the basket ended up.

So along with the heat of that day, came a most unexpected element of surprise. But who or what was most surprised - the cow, the dog, my brother George, me, or my Mother when she heard about my first flight, with a basket of apple peelings being my ticket to this unexpected flying adventure?

Suddenly the house did not feel so hot anymore. Indoors with Mom, Dad, my brothers and sisters seemed a safe place to be. And it would be many, many years before I got to fly again.

Buttered Toast, Tea and Stolen Afternoons

By Tony Myres

Holding tightly onto my mother's hand, we entered the big iron gates and started to go up the huge, stone steps at the top of which stood a gaunt, imposing, castle-like building. It looked like a prison but it was my boarding school, Queen Elizabeth's Hospital, and it was to be my place of residence - I couldn't bear to call it home - for the next seven years. At the top of the steps I said a brave but tearful goodbye to my mother and entered through an immense wooden door.

The thing that struck me first was the smell. I don't know what that smell really was - probably a combination of countless school dinners and the smell of well, just boys, that had impregnated the building over the centuries - but it never left me. Always, as I returned each term, that was the first thing that hit me and generated that knot of tension in my stomach that made me want to go back home again.

The boarders weren't allowed to meet their parents during the school week. Most of us lived in the city and we were allowed home only for Sunday afternoons and then only after an excruciatingly boring church service at which attendance was mandatory. For the new boys there was an added pain because for the first few weeks we were not allowed to go home at all on a Sunday. There was no explanation for this and I can only think it was thought to be like hardening seedlings so they would be better able to adapt and grow in a new environment. Although I think a more pragmatic reason was that many of us just wouldn't have come back to school after that first Sunday at home.

Despite the rules, my mother and I contrived to meet - not in a public place where I might be seen by a schoolmaster (there were no women teachers) or some snooping school prefect, but in the cafe of the local museum. "That'ull be one pown fifty, Luv". The voice of the waitress snapped me out of my reverie. It was 50 years on and I was sitting in the café of Bristol museum. As I fumbled in my pocket to find some one pound coins, I couldn't help thinking back again to those days with my mother. Buttered toast and tea never tasted so good as on those stolen afternoons at the Bristol Museum.

St. Anthony Revisited

By Tony Myres

My first, or Christian name as we used to call them in the pre-political correctness era, is Anthony, although I have always been known by the diminutive Tony.

At elementary school in Bristol, England in the late 1940s, children coined a wide variety of rhyming or mean sounding nicknames — like Timmy "FOUR EYES" or Billy "OWL" for children with spectacles. Children often had to endure all sorts of chants based on their name. You might think that not much could be done with the name Tony beyond the obvious Italian connection — being called Tony Boloni or Tonioni Macaroni. I did not really think there was any familial link with Italy even though I knew from my mother's marriage certificate that my absent, and to me unknown, American father's middle name was Angelo, which had an Italian ring to it. What I didn't know at that time, but discovered over forty years later, was that there really was Italian blood in me since my paternal great grandmother was born in Italy.

Kids can be incredibly inventive when it comes to names and making fun of them. It so happened that at this time in England there was a very funny comedian on BBC Radio, TV being almost unheard of among the working class at that time, whose name was Tony Hancock. So when it was my turn to be made the object of fun, I was encircled by a group of children chanting TOE-KNEE-HAND-COCK. With each word there would be gleeful pointing of fingers at the appropriate body part. While somewhat embarrassing, the latter was a useful introduction to sexual anatomy since at that time the only "cock" I knew about was the one in the Bible that crowed three times when Peter denied Jesus.

As I think back to those times I realize that my first name was not actually used very much to address me directly, even by my family. When thought to be out of earshot, or assumed to be engrossed in some playful activity, I would often hear myself referred to as "the boy".

When I went to boarding school at age eleven, it was unthinkable for any schoolmaster to address you by your first name. It was always by surname or, worse still, by number if the school marshal was involved. "Number 45 - change your band and 'ankerchief". Bands were the small white cravats that were an integral part of the Elizabethan uniform the boarders had to wear.

Boys at this age were very creative about names and there was much play on word sounds as well as word associations. Someone called S. Millbank, for example, would evolve through SMILL - BANK into SMELLY. Boys with surnames like Wood or Field would become TWIGGY and CORNY. Sometimes an epithet would be introduced between the first and last name such as the unfortunate Johnny "Cry Baby" Ray, named after a pop star of the time, Johnny Ray, whose hit song was all about crying over his lost love. We were all homesick as new boarders but it was fatal to let it show, as Ray did by his crying.

My own school nickname, which I acquired with some permanence when I was about thirteen, was MIZZ or MIZZY. The origins of this name related to an occasion when I absolutely refused to play soccer after tea in the schoolyard because I wanted to study my biology text book . For this I ended up being called a "swot", the common boyhood term for excessive studying. It was a rather critical game for the class team and I have to admit I was being a bit of a prig and I did let them down. So I not only became a "miserable sod" shortened to "MIZZ" (don't be such a MIZZ!), but also known as "SWOT" Myres. The latter did not last beyond that year for having gained the insultingly named Plodders Prize I reverted to form and just did enough to get by reasonably, but not outstandingly well, for the rest of my school career. The former name of MIZZ, having been said with some venom for a few weeks after the soccer game, soon elapsed into a sobriquet.

At University the use of first names, pure and simple, unadorned by fanciful descriptions at last became commonplace, at least among my peers, but professors would address one with strange formality as "Mister".

When I started work on my doctorate at another university, I remember being quite shocked to be addressed on first meeting one of my supervisors, an eminent scientist, as Tony. One of my other supervisors, a world authority on the nutrition of pigs, never seemed to address anyone by their first name except colleagues of a similar stature. In fact, when I left England having completed my PhD to do further research in Canada, letters from him always opened with "Dear Myres!" We lost touch for many years and reconnected by letter just before his death in 1997. His last letter addressed me as "Dear Tony". I felt I had arrived at last, recognized as an equal by the great guru of pig nutrition.

But where did my Christian name come from? The middle name, William, I could understand because it was my grandfather's name and there were other Williams in his ancestry. But Anthony? All my mother would say was, "Your dad really wanted it and so we decided on it." Since dad was not around, having left my nineteen-year-old mother when I was six months old, there was no checking to be done.

In middle age, I mulled this over many times, partly as a result of questions about my father from my own children. I knew I had been baptised in a Roman Catholic Church (Dad's influence again) but I had been brought up in the Church of England. Well, I thought, if it is the Roman Catholic influence, maybe I am named after a saint. Yes, that could be it — St. Anthony. I did a bit of research and thought that St. Anthony was the patron saint of children. Yes, yes, this was beginning to make sense. It would explain perhaps why I felt drawn to work in the 1970s on scientific and public health issues of relevance to children. I was spiritually linked with the saint himself. I even went so far, while at a scientific conference in 1990 in Padua, Italy, to visit and kiss the tomb of St. Anthony — to seal the deal as it were. Many years I later found out that St Anthony was not the patron saint of children since that honour belonged to St Nicholas. How could I not have known that! Perhaps I was just too focussed on making my own saintly links. I found out that there are two saints named Anthony.

Anthony the Abbot is regarded as the founder of monasticism although he spent most of his life living in solitude as a hermit..... no links there to me. Further research uncovered that the other saint, Anthony of Padua, is associated with the return of lost articles and missing persons. Now there is a connection in that. The standard Roman Catholic intercessionary prayer to St. Anthony is long and a bit arduous and I much prefer a Polish grandmother's version which went:

**Something's lost and can't be found
Please, St. Anthony, look around**

Although I never used that prayer-I didn't even know about it at the time. At the age of 48 years, I did find my father in Louisiana. After the initial joy and euphoria of having found one another, which is another story in itself, I asked him the question about my name. He sat back, looking reflective. Then, with a little smile, he leaned forward and said in his deep southern accent, "Well Son, yu know you wuz named afta a good 'ole boy called Anthony Marcello. He owned a bar down by the river and he give me mah first real job."

I was stunned. But a few more pieces of the puzzle began to fall into place for, on my parents' marriage license, my father's pre-war occupation was listed as "bartender". Furthermore, A. J. Marcello was the name on my baptism certificate as my godfather.

So that was it — named after the owner of a river-front bar in small town America. How the mighty are fallen! It was, perhaps, just as well that I had not mentioned to anyone my lofty aspirations to be linked with a saint.

The Cliff

By Barry W. Alder

She slowly opened her eyes, but saw nothing. Her mind was blank. Then she took a deep breath; and winced. Pain shot through the right side of her chest. She froze, waiting for the pain to subside. *Broken ribs*, she thought, taking a measured, shallow breath. As the pain slowly receded, she remembered what had happened.

She'd been at the cliff edge, searching for berries. She thought she'd been careful, but in retrospect, not careful enough. A stone she'd stepped on had slipped, and she'd gone over. That was late afternoon, and now it was dark. She wondered how she could have survived the fall. The cliff face had been at least a hundred feet high where she'd been and there was no way she could have survived that.

And yet she was still alive. Flat on her back and hurt, but alive.

Can't stay here, she thought as she carefully moved her fingers and toes to see if she could feel them. No pain and she could feel the movement. She moved her arms next, generating a shot of pain in her chest, but nowhere else.

Now for the big test, she thought as she moved her legs slightly. Another shot of chest pain, but, this time, severe pain in her right thigh as well.

"That sucks," she hissed through her teeth and forced her leg muscles to relax.

She lay there, quiet for a long time, willing herself to relax, breathing slowly, and staring at the dark, cloud-covered sky.

Finally, she decided to move, to at least try to sit up so she could see her surroundings. Very carefully, she twisted to her left, fighting the pain and forcing her torso up to a sitting position. She held that position, gasping between clenched teeth until the pain was down to a tolerable level and she could breathe almost normally.

She looked around, but saw nothing. The clouds hid whatever faint light the stars and the new moon might have provided.

The night was cool and she began to shiver

I need to find some shelter, she thought. *I won't last the night exposed like this.*

As if to answer her unspoken fears, she heard the nearby howls of two wolves. A chill ran down her spine, reinforcing her resolve to move. She placed her hands behind her and gingerly pulled herself back, trying to ignore the pain in her side and leg. She paused for a moment, composing herself for the next attempt. Shifting her weight to the left, she jerked her right hand backward and struck solid stone. The shock caused her to thrust her hand down hard, scraping it on the rocks, and she let out a scream of pain. After a few moments, the pain subsided and she forced herself to a more forward sitting position, freeing her hands to explore. She soon discovered she had backed into a wall of rock, solid for as far as she could feel.

So much for that direction, she thought wryly. *Guess I'll have to go along the rock.*

She was just about to pull herself to the left when the cloud cover broke. There was not enough light to see clearly, but she could just make out the ground around her, fading gently into total darkness to her right and in front of her but making an abrupt line about three feet from where she was on her left.

She stared at the clear delineation before her, trying to comprehend what it meant. It slowly dawned on her that it meant there was nothing in the darkness, that the earth stopped at that line.

She let herself down and moved to the line. There was no change in it the closer she got, and she stopped a few inches from it. By this time her heart was racing with the fear that had been building with every inch she moved closer to it. She reached her trembling hand toward the darkness and slowly dropped it, the faint light giving it a ghostly sheen. Her hand dropped below the ground level and kept going, stopping only when her arm hit the ground at the line.

The realization came to her slowly. She hadn't fallen all the way down the cliff. She'd landed on a ledge part way down. She leaned back against the rock, mind numb.

The sun was well up when she woke abruptly. She didn't remember falling asleep and the thought shocked her, and the sudden movement brought a sharp stab of pain to her side. Once the pain subsided, she looked to see where the sun was in the sky, trying to determine what time it was.

'Bout ten, she thought sadly, slowly looking around. In the full sunlight, she could see the edges of her limited domain. Five feet to her right, five feet in front of her, and about a foot to her left. Then she looked up. It was difficult to see clearly, but she thought she was about twenty feet down from the top. *And about eighty feet up from the valley bottom*, she thought.

She closed her eyes, trying to decide what to do. On the plus side, it was near peak season for summer hikers. However, she was in one of the more remote parts of the park, by her own choice. There was a chance someone might spot her if she stayed put. She could see the small river below, not too far from the base of the cliff. She knew that canoeists sometimes took the waterway to the campground about five miles upstream. She was positive she could yell enough to catch their attention if they went by.

But when would they go by, she wondered. If someone was heading for the campground, it could be anytime; now or five hours from now.

"Nothing I can do right now," she murmured to herself. She tried to reposition herself such that she was comfortable and could easily see the river, but gave up after fifteen minutes. Sitting put too much pressure on her broken leg causing the broken bones to push together. Lying helped the leg immensely, but severely restricted her view of the river, and neither position provided relief from the rough stones on the ledge for long.

The day passed slowly. The hot sun beating down made her acutely aware of her lack of water and shade. She drifted in and out of daydreaming, scolding herself for not paying closer attention to the river. But every time she looked, she saw nothing.

By sunset, she could hardly swallow, her mouth was so dry. The hunger pains that had periodically stirred her from her daydreams had thankfully stopped, but had been replaced with a deep throbbing in her right thigh. It had been growing worse all day, and as she now looked at it, she realized it had swollen badly. She wasn't sure if that was a good thing or bad, but knew that she had to get it looked at soon. Her life depended on it.

With a great effort, she rolled on to her stomach and pulled herself to the edge of the ledge. In the fading light, she cursed herself for not having done it sooner. The long shadows hid the details she was desperately searching for. She painfully moved herself back from the edge. Trying to find a comfortable spot to sleep for the night.

Sleep came fitfully, the pain in her thigh a constant companion. She took some thanks in the heavy cloud cover that kept the night warm, despite her light clothing.

She awoke shortly after dawn, her leg in more pain from the swelling than from the break. Looking down at the river, she desperately hoped to spot a canoe or another hiker, but saw nothing. She started to cry.

I don't want to die here, she thought. *I have to get down.*

Pulling herself back to the edge, she cleared her eyes and looked down. The morning sun favored her and she could clearly see all the way down. Her heart fell. There didn't seem any way down. She was about to give up when a small bird flew past her and landed on a small bush outcropping.

Maybe. Just maybe, she thought as her eyes followed a possible path down.

But it was so far down, and she felt so weak.

"I don't know if I can make it", she whispered to herself, "but I can't stay here and die. I have to try."

She took a deep breath and eased herself to the edge. She carefully positioned herself so she could shift into a climbing position, slipped her legs over the edge, and screamed.

Three Dog Tales

by Kathi Nidd

Blitzen

Overcome by the smell from years of strays ingrained in every inch of the shelter, I entered guardedly and stared down the dimly lit hallway between the cages. The door clunked behind me and stirred the happenstance pack. They began to whimper, then bark, then shriek with delight. For the door opening meant one of two things for the poor homeless dogs; food or a walk, and both were always welcome.

It was my first day as a volunteer for the Ottawa Humane Society. After several months of pondering to which organization I wanted to dedicate my time, I had decided on walking stray dogs. This was a mutually beneficial opportunity as it meant I got exercise while spending some time with the poor pups. My friends wondered why I had taken so long to come to the obvious conclusion, for my love of dogs was undeniable. That morning I underwent my training and I was now ready to walk my very first dog! Since they all needed walking, I was free to choose whichever dog I wanted from the vast sea of eyes monitoring my every move.

My head moved from right to left, from pit bulls to spaniels, each one begging me for attention. Suddenly, directly in front of me, I saw a blob of white, rising and falling as though on a trampoline. The dog, at least I think it was a dog, was ... bouncing. Two feet tall and a mass of white hair, the Eskimo dog rose and fell gently on his four spindly legs like a blanket being fluffed on a bed. I watched him bounce, up and down, so gracefully and without even bending his legs, and I was taken. Within minutes, Blitzen and I were out in the January snow enjoying the sparkle of the afternoon sun. He never slowed down, even after our long walk together. When I returned him to his cage so I could take another dog, Blitzen paused for just a moment and stared at me in thanks. Then he began to bounce again. I am convinced he did not want the next volunteer to know that he'd already been walked, so he began his sales pitch all over again.

For the next six months, I returned to the shelter twice a week to walk dogs and, unfortunately, every time I opened the large clunky door "my boy" was waiting for me, bouncing. Dogs would come and go, while Blitzen became a fixture. High energy, he was being passed up by all the potential adopters but luckily, as a no kill shelter, it was only a matter of time. I would have taken him myself were it not for my own aging Jack Russell who was too set in her ways for a brother. Blitzen was always the first dog I walked, assuming another volunteer hadn't taken him already. And even if they had, I'd spare him a few extra minutes at the end of my shift.

Then one day I stared at his cage and a large black shepherd lab cross stared back at me, not bouncing. Blitzen was gone! The shelter staff informed me he'd been adopted by a young couple who were both runners. I envisioned "my boy" running every day with his new family and I was overjoyed for him. I continued volunteering for another two and a half years after that, but no dog ever replaced the love I felt for "my boy Blitzen".

Brutus

About a year into my volunteering, I was used to handling the dogs that were, well …. difficult! I had become an expert at handling those who jumped and pulled on their leashes or those who did not seem to understand their own strength. These were the dogs that were gently listed as "in need of a loving family who can provide training". One clear autumn Saturday morning, I harnessed up Brutus, a two-year-old husky, for a quick jaunt around the block. I could feel my arm muscles elongating as we headed down the street. And when Brutus saw other dogs, it was all I could do to keep my feet planted on the ground. I pictured myself being lifted like a kite and pulled by the enormous strength and energy of the dog. Obviously he wasn't trying to hurt me but merely demonstrate to me that he could be a champion sled puller! I understood, yet tried in vain to revert to my lessons on dog training from the books and videos I had utilized. Unfortunately, Brutus hadn't read the books nor seen the videos, so eventually I just glided along defeated, leash grasped by two hands, willing the walk to come to a quick end.

The Ottawa shelter is located in a fairly busy neighbourhood and reluctantly I had to turn up a very busy street as a shortcut to get Brutus back home. Car and pedestrian traffic whizzed by as I managed to keep him on the sidewalk with a very short lead. Proud of myself, I actually thought we'd made it as I managed to lead him behind a group of people who were waiting for the bus. Silly me! Brutus had another idea and decided to follow them. As the bus pulled up and opened its doors, the passengers, followed by Brutus, flowed towards the door. I felt the leash pull left and, then to my distress, I watched Brutus board the bus!

I was left with two choices; follow Brutus on to the bus and explain to the frustrated driver that we needed off at the next stop or let go of the leash and leave Brutus on his own without fare to travel the streets of Ottawa! Finally, just prior to the doors closing, I managed to pull him back to the street before the bus moved away. I sat, laughing, on the bus stop bench and petted Brutus behind the ears. The passengers stared out the windows at Brutus and me laughing as the bus drove away. I did not share my story with the shelter staff. It was our little secret.

I never learned of Brutus' fate but I hope he found a family in the country away from public transportation!

Cody

Towards the end of my volunteer days at the shelter, I had the unique situation occur where one of the shelter dogs had previously been owned by a colleague of mine, Dan. Dan had given Cody away as he could no longer keep him in his new apartment building. Old, overweight, and without any of the puppy-like enthusiasm that translates to adoptable, Cody had taken over one of the larger corner cages at the shelter. As a favour, I told Dan that I would check on him every time I was there.

One Sunday afternoon, after working all morning, I took Cody for a walk. We did not go far, for it was only a half block before he looked at me with his elderly eyes as if to say "enough." Returning to the shelter I evaluated the pack, a particularly small group that day and realized everyone had been walked. I returned Cody to his cage and locked the door. Like a large beige couch, he stood solid in the cage. I looked at his knowing face as he tried to tell me his story. His puppy and young adult life had been full and wonderful and now, what was left?

On a whim, I re-opened the cage and stepped inside. Cody immediately lay down on his blanket, his huge jowls overlapping on my foot. Defeated, I put my coat down on the cage floor and sat next to him. I'm not sure if it was out of friendship for Dan or of love for this lump of a dog; but I decided to stay a while. As we rested peacefully, the cage door began to swing open on its own momentum so eventually I reached my hand through and locked myself in from the other side. Together, Cody and I lay, listening to the other dogs' chatter fade from yapping to murmurs to sleep. And, eventually, my long day overcame me and I too fell asleep on top of Cody's lumpy neck.

I don't know who was more surprised, me when I woke up locked in a dog cage or the shelter staff who came around the corner and found me asleep, locked in a cage and ready for dinner! I'm not sure how long Cody lasted or if he ever found a good home but I do know we gave the shelter staff a great story that afternoon.

* * *

A life of career travel and other commitments took me away from my volunteering at the shelter but I do hope to return again someday. On the surface it appears that we do it for the dogs; making their lives more fulfilled and happy but the dogs and I know the truth.

Granny's Last Stand at Badminton Road

by Tony Myres

I shall never forget the look on Granny's face as the doctor asked her, in what I thought was a rather patronizing tone, "Now, Mrs. Brain, can you tell me the name of the Prime Minister of England?"

Granny was 89 years old and the doctor was doing some preliminary testing to determine Granny's state of mind and to help us (myself, my mother and my wife) decide if it was time for her to go into some form of permanent care outside of home.

The year was 1972 and my wife and I were back in England on a short Christmas visit from Canada to show off our three month old first baby to my mother, my grandmother and my great uncle. When I knocked on the front door of the terraced house that had been the family home since 1926, we were greeted by my mother in tears. She was not only embarrassed by the mess the house was in but also afraid of what Granny might do because she was often unpredictable. I think she was afraid, too, of letting us see that Granny had come to this state and how we would react.

Rita and I had been in Canada since 1970 and during that time Granny had slipped slowly into senility, and Mum had never told us in the letters how bad things really were for her. I dearly loved my grandmother as did my mother for, in a sense, we owed our lives to her. Mum had been a 19 year old single mother and I was the "war baby" and there was no father around. He was an American GI who mysteriously "disappeared" after D-Day. It was Granny who took us in and, in effect, raised me from the age of two as Mum had to go back to work in order to make her contribution to the upkeep of Granny's home. Mum, who never remarried, worked continuously in a variety of jobs until 1970, when she gave up work to take care of

Granny full time at home. Now it was too much for her.

I looked across the room at Granny sitting in the same wing chair in the same corner of the room where she had always sat as long as I could remember. We were all waiting intently for her answer to Dr. Persil's question. I found it hard to believe that this was my Granny being put in a different kind of corner like this. She had been such a powerful figure in my life, the Victorian matriarch who ruled the roost at 37 Badminton Road, Bristol. This was the person who had lived through the First World War suffering terrible family losses in it, the same indomitable spirit emerged unbroken from the depression of the 1930s - the "terrible low decade" as Auden called it, and she survived the bombing of Bristol during the Blitz. This was my Granny who more than once, when I was a little boy, saved me from the bullies of Badminton Road. I can still see her standing on the top front step outside the front door speaking imperiously to one of the street bullies and ordering him (with me hiding behind her) –"You go up and play by yer own place and don't be such a bully!" This was the same Granny who took me every day by bus to Ashley Down Infants School for kindergarten, who took me to grammar school entrance exams when I was eleven years old, who traveled to Leeds University in 1967 to attend my graduation and later that year to Hitchin to attend the my wedding. Now this wonderful old lady who had survived so much had her back to the wall in her own house and was facing a sort of Dunkirk; but there was no way out of this one.

How would she answer? Half of me wanted her to get the right answer so she would not feel humiliated, and half of me wanted her to get it wrong so that we could begin the process of putting her into care and so lift the caring burden from my Mum. Granny was clutching her crocodile handbag - her pride and joy when I was young and only used on special occasions - but now in an advanced state of breakdown. Gone were the days when it would contain bundles of fivers (five pound notes). "Well….. I always like to have a bit of money on me," she would say. Now it would be a little bit of Monopoly money that my Mum had long ago substituted for the real thing.

Granny's face was a mixture of self satisfaction and disdain. She leant forward and placed her handbag at the side of the chair and then sat back, folded her arthritic hands in her lap, looked across at the doctor and said, with a glint in her eye, "Well, well, well-dew mean to tell me that you - a doctor with all your education - and you don't know the answer to that! Hmm" and with that she leant back, closed her eyes, smiled a beautiful smile, and settled down to sleep.

There was a voice inside me wanting to burst out. I wanted to punch the air and shout, "YES! Yes! That's my Granny. You tell 'em Granny!" But, of course, I did not. Although outwardly I was so pleased that she didn't go down without a fight, I knew in my heart that it was now the beginning of the end for Granny. Not long after our return to Canada, Granny was moved into a geriatric hospital and a few months later I was back in Bristol to attend her funeral.

The Granny Suite

by Rita Myres

There are as many reasons for falling in love with a house as there are house hunters. For myself and my husband, Tony, searching for a new home to accommodate our growing family, it was the granny suite that clinched the deal. We had moved to our current home, a 3-bedroom bungalow, when our first son was a blond, two-year-old with limitless energy. Now it was ten years later, and we had welcomed a second son and a daughter into our family, as well as Tony's mother, Norma. She had joined us here in Canada, emigrating from England after a prolonged stint as caregiver for her mother and then her uncle, which had left her exhausted and without close family.

Our bungalow, seemingly so spacious when we first moved in, was now bursting at the seams. It was time to move and, for me, the prospect generated excitement and also a little sadness. The idea of relocating took on the weight of reality after we contacted a neighbour who was a real estate agent. Soon after that, twelve other agents from her company came through our home. It was a bizarre experience to hear them dispassionately discussing the selling points as well as the limiting features of our home, the place that was the centre of our universe. We couldn't know, on this day, that it would be six months before our bungalow would be sold; six months of phone calls that interrupted nap-time or dinner, with a request for a viewing; six months of being on "tidy up" alert and of coming to dread the emptying of the Lego containers on the sitting room rug; six months of being out-of-sync with myself as a go-with-the-flow mother, who viewed a messy house as a sign that I made my children's needs the priority; six months that ended when we finally moved all of us into the house with the granny suite.

I use the word "finally" because we had found and purchased our next home almost a year before we moved into it. At the time we bought it, it was a rental property complete with tenants, and we became somewhat reluctant and completely inexperienced landlords until the leases expired, almost a year later. We had looked at a lot of other houses before settling on this one. Something about it appealed to our English sensibilities. It had the ambiance of history, having been built early in the 20th century. We were curious about its origins, who had built it, and how it had subsequently been adapted by its previous owners. Contained within its three floors were three separate apartments and we were excited about the possibilities for reorganizing the space to fit our three-generation family. The house was set within a sizable garden, which offered the potential for flower beds, summer cricket games and maybe even a frozen pond for winter games of hockey! There were porches, a sun room and a summer kitchen.......... places to find solitude with a good book.

Between them, the current tenants and the absent owners had gently neglected the house, as evidenced by the too-long grass, the missing light bulbs on the stairways and the collapsing summer kitchen at the back of the house. There was a slightly down-at-heel, in-need-of-being-cherished feel about the house that challenged us to put our mark on it, to make it our own.

The lease for the third floor apartment was the first to expire and, after the tenants moved out, we set about cleaning and painting it, making it fresh and welcoming for Norma, my mother-in-law. On a warm, August day we moved her in. The arrangements worked well, despite the challenge of negotiating two 180 degree turns on the staircase with a sizable couch and Norma's highly prized rosewood and glass china cabinet, passed down to her by her own mother. At day's end she was completely ensconced and almost completely unpacked. It had taken both of us, Tony and myself, with "assistance" from our three children and a moving crew of two men, to accomplish the relocation of one highly anxious and very particular older lady. We were congratulating ourselves on a job well done after dinner that evening, with our children in bed and our feet up, when the phone rang. It was Norma, calling from the second floor tenant's apartment to say that she had taken some empty cardboard boxes down to the basement and that, while she was down there, a mischievous gust of wind blew through the house and slammed shut her apartment door. She had not taken her key with her and now was locked out of her new home! With good grace, my good husband hauled himself out of his armchair and cycled over to the house with his key to let her back inside the granny suite.

One month later, the remaining two leases expired and, despite the fact that our bungalow still had not sold, we decided to take a leap of faith and bring our family to join Norma into the house with the granny suite. Within a week of leaving it, we had received two offers to purchase the bungalow, confirming our decision to reunite our family. The page of life had turned and the granny suite on the third floor was Norma's home within our home for thirteen years, until December 1997.

Story For Dreyden

by Chantal Frobel

Staring through the window, I am a young girl watching the snow flakes slowly fall and glisten on the ground. My aunt is patiently watching me as she sits by the phone. This beautiful blanket of bright snow is the perfect homecoming for your arrival. My new baby sister is born on this March day, and I am eager to finally have a best friend in my life to grow up with in good times, and in bad times. My sister became a blessing. Once she entered my life we were never drawn apart.

The years have passed and both of us are now young adults who have forged a strong and courageous relationship. These memories of your birth are a stream flowing through my mind as if it were just yesterday as I sit alone again in the waiting area of the third floor birthing unit. My very own baby sister is now welcoming her first and precious baby boy into this world. Like a tiny flower waiting to blossom, I know your mother will nurture and care for you in the most loving way. I am honoured to be your godmother and promise to encourage you in all that life has to offer. As I sit and wait, the butterflies are fluttering around my heart, and I am anxious to hear word that you have been born.

Suddenly, without warning, I hear those fateful words announced on the hospital intercom "Code two labour and delivery." The words echoed a constant replay in my mind. I felt as though time was frozen. I was in a panic, and felt my heart crumbling as a flash of fear drained all my energy and I now felt completely numb. I was in a dream. Marshalling the strength within me, I ran out of the waiting room and down the hall to my baby sister's hospital room. With each step I took, I was praying to our angels for my baby sister's safe and joyful delivery of her new baby boy into the awaiting world. To hear you cry, to see you smile in your mother's arms was my only wish on that April morning.

    I stopped in front of the hospital room as I was told to wait there by the nurse. The door was closed and the silence was too much to bear. It seemed as if time stood still. Finally, as if from the heavens above, I heard the cries of glee and the door opened! I saw you wrapped gently within your mother's arms and happiness filled the air. As I looked down upon you, this tiny gift from God, I could already imagine your ideas and thoughts shining in your eyes. As your godmother I wished for your hopes and dreams to soar as high as the blueness of the skies.

My Path to Happiness

by Kit Flynn

A Dream

When I was little, my dream - actually, my unquestioned assumption - was that I would grow up, get married, have a wonderful loving marriage and family, be an important business person like my Dad, and that I could 'make' myself a happy life.

Today, about half way through life, I can honestly say that a happy life is what I have. Was it always this way? Heck no. As for all the rest, well, what I didn't know then was that my will and desire weren't the only factors at play. Dreams, I found out, had a way of changing - and that was OK, too. Living with gratitude, letting go of my resentments, living without being weighed down with regret, loving as much as I can, owning my choices, staying in the present as I grow each day older have all been important ideas allowing me to find and then to maintain the happiness I enjoy today.

In my life so far, there have been factors such as; uncontrollable situations, bad luck, mistakes, biological realities, the unrelenting demands of the heart and the body, my own shortcomings and other people's energy - all of which have affected my childhood master plan for happiness and fulfillment.

But leading a happy and genuine life - I am, despite it all, or in fact, because of it all. How I define happiness, I am realizing, has changed over the course of my life. It is an ever evolving concept. Being grateful for what IS instead of responding to life as a victim of circumstance helped me to take the first step towards finding genuine happiness.

Gratitude

It is difficult to truly turn negative thoughts and dark perceptions into something positive. To take one life example, when I was a child, I was parented by an alcoholic father and a co-dependent mother. It used to seem like an insurmountable endeavor to consider my childhood a blessing.

My family of origin was a 'normal' alcoholic family by all accounts. My parents moved us around every couple of years or so and by the time I was 20 I had had 16 different bedrooms. There were many violent incidents in our home. Financial security fluctuated wildly. I found myself reverse parenting at times and felt affected by constant upheaval causing me to live in chaos and to have deep rooted feelings of abandonment, rejection and betrayal. All this led to hurt and anger. Was it possible to feel genuine gratitude for my childhood - even when I was told that it may help to open the way to living a happy life?

Yes! I began to notice and then to appreciate all that I did have and started looking at the positive aspects of the people, places and things in my life. I had had an abundant childhood in many unconventional ways and I could choose to feel gratitude for those things. I began to appreciate my father and feel the immense love that I hold for him and I learned how to separate that from the alcoholic man dependent on his booze. I learned to reframe my expectations and focus on the positive aspects of my mother. This allowed me the space to love her and respect her for who she is and for doing her very best for me.

To feel genuine gratitude, I took a look at my childhood. I chose to build up new beliefs and go forward being the person I really am - not the person who was living from an old childish, outdated belief system. I began to apply my very best thinking to myself, starting with gratitude for all that was and is beautiful about life.

When I focused on gratitude, I felt it's grace leading to a calm happiness. I apply the same concepts to all things now and it has become a habit. This continues to lay the foundation for my serene life today.

I noticed that once I changed and once gratitude became automatic, life got better, happier. Now my attention was directed to the heavy sack of resentments I was carrying around. They, too, were keeping me from the happiness I sought.

> " When I focus on what's good, I have a good day. When I focus on what's bad, I have a bad day."
> Anonymous

Resentments

The 'good-girl', 'the fixer', 'the dependable one' were some of my roles which helped shape my early identity and self worth. Moreover, they set me up on a destructive course leading to big resentments of people, places and things. I didn't know who I was or what I wanted and it didn't occur to me to ask. These resentments caused unpredictable behaviour, and confused me as well as those around me.

How do we not carry the burden of resentments? How do we let go of them in pursuit of simple happiness? In my life, it was as a result of a couple of key realizations:

People pleasers are liars. If I was going to live a genuine and truly happy life, everyone I met was not going to like me. This was a horribly hard concept since I was used to defining myself by what others thought of me and my ability to help them. I had to get to know the real me, be willing to stand up for me, be able to ask to have my needs met and let the proverbial chips fall where they may.

Resentments only hurt the people who hold them. I was self-torturing and the main question was why? Why did I feel that the burden and destructiveness of resentments was what I deserved? If I had to only choose to be true to who I am and let resentments go then why not choose it?

These questions led me to realize that experiences in my life, derived from life events that were out of my control, had hard wired my attitude that I didn't deserve happiness. This established core belief was supported when my 42 year old husband was given a stage 4 cancer diagnosis and died 13 months later.

Other significant losses just prior to my husband's death had begun the pattern of loss and abandonment. I experienced 6 close family deaths in nine months. (My thoughts: why did I have to lose my dad at 58, a parent-in-law, two grandparents, a friend and - a pregnancy?). Why did my father-in-law have to die just 6 months before his son, my husband John? Why did a shocking total of 8 close relatives die leaving me feeling like my family had been annihilated? Most of all, why did the two innocent and adorable children of mine have to be without John and fatherless at 5 and 7 years old?

So much to feel resentful about - but who was I to blame? The only answer that made sense was me. After all, my childhood fantasy had started to come true. I had met a wonderful man, married him and started a warm loving family. Did I think I just simply didn't deserve to have such happiness?

Yes, unfortunately. And I started to change that thinking when I started to seek happiness. I chose not to feel hurt. I chose not to be a victim any longer. I chose to find out who I was and then live life from that place. Attachments to resentments only fueled the delay of uncovering my genuine self, just as I found out, attachments to regrets would do as well.

"Hurt People, hurt people" - Anonymous

Regrets

Lucky, we are, when our mistakes can be undone or atoned for, promptly put aside and us being made the wiser for them. To live happily, could I think the same way about mistakes that were big and permanently life changing?

Yes! To live happy and fulfilled, I had to look at some big mistakes and place them in my thinking and into my heart as a sincere and important feedback, not failure, a launching pad into my deeper understanding of life. I had to look at what holding onto the feelings about my regrets was doing for me. Why was I choosing not to forgive myself? Were they all in fact 'mistakes' or were they actions decided upon with the best of honest intentions with what I knew at the time?

Soon after the death of my first husband, I met a man who initially made me very happy. He didn't seem scared off by the fact that I came with two little boys and we began seeing each other. I had an eerie feeling of familiarity with him. Oddly, I found myself comforted by the confusing signals and by walking on eggshells in our home. I realize now that my home situation conveniently distracted me from my overwhelming grief over John's death. I felt safe in an odd kind of way dealing with familiar issues since death and loss was something new and horrifying. In this new relationship, putting on false fronts for others' sake, keeping secrets, multiple compulsions in the home, ridicule and sarcasm were all familiar from my long-ago past.

Upon my request, he legally adopted my boys, because at that time, I was terribly afraid that I, too, would die leaving my boys orphans. I eventually married this man only to realize quite quickly that I had sought out and married someone who reminded me, at times, of my father. After seeking help and support, I gained the courage to scoop up my young-teen boys and to begin to live a simplified life without confusion, meanness and disharmony.

At first, the feeling of regret was keeping me very low until I realized that the choices I had made were with the very best of intentions. Initially, I was with him for my children and myself and I also ended the marriage for my children and myself. It took me a while to realize that my childhood feelings of chaos were familiar and I sought out the familiar at this time of deep loss. It was 100% understandable, given my life's experiences. All I had to do was choose to forgive myself and be understanding and to choose to let go of torturing myself over regrettable decisions made in the past.

Finding happiness by letting ourselves off our own hooks, shredding regrets once identified and understood, leads to happiness and the ability to live a full life. Love was what came next in my goal to find happiness. I knew it was important but I didn't realize just how incredibly important it was.

> " Acceptance - is the answer to all my problems today. "
> Anonymous

Love

Love is what matters. It is the main thing. Learning about love is a wondrous journey. Love for me had to be found in myself for myself, from the Divine and towards all others. It wasn't a linear process, rather it all happened simultaneously and the result was the blissful 'falling in love' feeling. It continues to this day.

The feeling of non-ego centered love I now live with is permanent. I don't just hope for love - I know it. I feel no question about whether it will fail me with the next inevitable big life experience I'll be faced with. Love will never fail me, my relationship with the Divine is permanent and I will always have a deep feeling of love, forgiveness and non-judgment for my fellow human beings. This confidence in love may be the biggest, most important factor in my solid continuing happiness today.

How did I learn this? How did it grow? At one point of my life, I had a choice. To love or to hate. Hate would tear me apart and delay the happiness I sought. It would take the same amount of energy as love, so I chose to focus on love.

A dilemma was presented to me when my teenage sons chose to move out of my home and in with my second husband. The months preceding their decision were difficult for my sons because my ex-husband did not want to have any contact with me. It was a very stressful time for them.

So, from my point of view, when they were presented with the option of living in an environment with few rules, a large extended family and lots of financial perks which included a ski chalet, lap top computers and Caribbean holidays it became an easy decision for two teenagers. Fortunately, I was strong enough, at that time in my life, to know that I would continue to love my children no matter what and not give my ex-husband the power to come between us.

By learning to truly love myself, the Divine and the world around me, I was able to learn to take a long term perspective on this situation, to trust that the universe was exactly the way it was supposed to be. I didn't know the reason, but I knew that love was the foundation.

Words like betrayal, loyalty, selfishness and hate were replaced by the feelings of understanding, love and peace. Long term perspectives could be fathomed and then lived, with trust in love.

Happiness is a natural outcome of a life lived with love at it's core. The choice to choose love is a power we all have. Many other choices will shape the degree to which we live in serenity. We can choose how we think and what we do and then live at peace with ourselves.

"Nothing, absolutely nothing happens in God's world by mistake."
Anonymous

Choices

Five years ago I was overweight and unhappy about it. I began to notice that all the talk in my head was hurtful and only served to make me feel badly about myself. I realized that I could continue the war with my weight and keep doing the same things I had done for years, or I could change the way I talk to myself. The choice was mine.

Choosing to say positive, goal enhancing things to myself changed everything. I lost almost 50 pounds and do not live the same way I used to. Food is now delicious fuel for this strong dependable body of mine and I feed it with just the right amount of healthy foods it needs. Gone are the days I ate to fill holes that had nothing to do with being hungry.

Our resources are finite. We have only so much time, energy and money. This means that the precious time we spend catastrophizing, obsessively analyzing and putting ourselves down, with negative self-talk, and worrying, is a choice we are making. This energy inevitably leads us to exactly that which we fear.

When I started to see how my thought choices were negatively affecting my happiness, I realized I had better use my energy differently and began to change it up. I quickly noticed that positive thoughts led to positive outcomes.

In my weight example, choosing negative thoughts, such as "I can't do it", "I will always yo-yo", "I have no self-control", "I am fat and ugly" kept me overweight at war with my weight. Now I try to stop all my negative self-talk in its tracks. I visualize a large red stop sign when I notice a negative thought. I quickly change it to a random positive one without a full analysis of how I got there in the first place.

Stopping the spiral downward has been a key to controlling my destructive self thoughts and replacing them with positive, goal reaching, life enhancing, positive ones. These choices have been life changing in many areas besides weight. Replacing self destructive thoughts can lead the way to all your dreams coming true.

If it takes the same energy and time to think of a horrible outcome as it does a possible positive outcome, let's get to happiness by using the positive energy and increasing the likelihood of the positive result. We can try it one thought at a time. With practice it does get easier and the results are truly amazing!

We have to be in the present moment to catch ourselves with negative thoughts that we choose to change into positive ones. Being in the present moment and setting achievable short term, attainable goals has ensured ongoing peace and happiness.

" You can choose to reside in a place of fear, a place where you doubt who you are and what you are capable of OR you can choose to believe in the best version of yourself."
unknown

Future Moments

Living each moment in each day the best way I can is the way I make my way into my happy future. Worry in general and worry about the future specifically, has significantly decreased in my life. I have an overwhelming, solid belief that the future can be trusted and that my human brain must not mess with the universe's master plan. I'll do my part, yes - but I just have to get it going, I don't have to get it right!

Having chosen to try to let go of the all-or-nothing extreme thinking I had lived with most of my life, I now decide what things need my attention (such as bills, financial plans, making my annual doctors' and dentist's appointments) and what things do not, and trust that everything else will be dealt with, if they are important, as they come up. I don't try to mind-read my loved ones and friends and encourage them to ask me for what they need. Life today is simple.

"It is never too late to be what you might have been."
George Elliot

A Dream Fulfilled

The happiness that now fills my life came to me bit by bit, one day at a time as a result of some dedicated work.

I have found true happiness, first, by allowing myself to have dreams and expectations for my life, then to work on feeling gratitude for all the good things and experiences. All the while, working on understanding and reducing the negative impact of the resentments I carried around. I also came to accept that regrets are a part of life and it is OK to regret things as long as you are able to forgive yourself for decisions you have made.

The next important influence on my happiness is the work I invested in the pursuit of love. What I mean by that is the discovery that love starts within ourselves and then can be directed outward. Once the concept of love was fully integrated, the element of choices came into play. Each of us has the right to make unique choices which will influence how we live and enjoy our lives. Making positive choices on how to think will lay a path towards a productive and fulfilled future, which in turn will provide us with a well deserved, happy life.

Perhaps even a version of our childhood dream will come true - just in a different form and possibly, even better than ever imagined!

Rescue at Green Lake

by Barry W. Alder

It was the silence that woke him. No noise whatsoever. He slowly realized he was lying on his back, looking up at the stars through the leaf bare trees. The air was crystal clear and the stars danced far above. He was breathing easily and felt calm, but something in the back of his mind said that this was wrong.

I shouldn't be here, he thought. *But where should I be?*

Gradually, a sound made its way to his consciousness; the faint forlorn sound of ice coated branches hitting each other in the slight breeze. He strained to hear more, but nothing came. Then he saw his breath.

He gradually became aware of a numbing cold seeping through the back of his light jacket and his pant legs.

Winter, he thought slowly. *January deep freeze.*

What am I doing here?

He tried to think of what had just happened, but nothing came.

Another sound, creaking, came from his right. He turned his head, wincing as a shot of pain momentarily blinded him, to look.

A car. Upside down. Roof crushed.

His car.

The memories came flooding back. He was on his way home. There must have been ice on that last corner. He'd lost control, went over the embankment, and flipped.

A mild panic overcame him and he tried to get up, but his body was slow to respond. Eventually he sat up and looked around.

There was only the light of the quarter moon, but that was more than enough to see his surroundings.

What was the temperature?

He recalled hearing minus twenty-five on the radio just as he left.

I'm not dressed for that, he thought apprehensively. *Now what?*

I can't stay here. Nobody will be down this road 'til morning.

It slowly dawned on him. The nearest house he could remember seeing was over twenty kilometers away, back up the hill. Down the hill it was fifty kilometers to the next town.

Maybe if I stay in the car. It might be warmer.

Just then he heard a low growl to his left.

Not twenty feet from him were two wolves, staring. He froze, fear creeping through him.

Shit, he thought. *Gotta move.*

He struggled to his feet and looked at the wolves. They hadn't moved.

"What do you want?" he yelled, faking a confidence he didn't feel. "Go away! I'm not your supper!"

The wolves didn't move.

Maybe I can scare them away, he thought desperately, and took a step towards them.

They didn't move, but growled and bared their fangs.

He stopped.

This isn't working, he thought as he took a step back.

He knew he couldn't outrun them, and he knew he couldn't fight them. Slowly, he backed up toward the car, watching the wolves closely.

They hadn't moved.

He felt the car against his back.

Now what?

As he stared at the wolves, they moved to his right, closer to the road.

I can't stay here. I'll freeze to death.

The wolves moved closer, and his heart began to race.

Or be wolf meat.

The wolves continued their advance.

Shit, he thought frantically looking around. *Maybe I can lose them in the bush.*

He laughed out loud.

The wolves stopped.

You're a freaking idiot. You can't lose them. They can smell you.

But maybe. They can't be that hungry or they would have attacked by now. Maybe they'll lose interest in me if I make it hard for them.

He watched as one of the wolves moved farther to his right.

Great! Now I'm completely blocked off from the road.

He scanned to his left. There was only bush; his only remaining option.

He took a deep breath and started trudging through the knee high snow to the bush. After a few steps he stopped.

This is stupid, he thought. *I can't even walk fast in this snow.*

He looked back at the wolves. They hadn't moved, so he continued.

He reached the bush and found the snow a lot more shallow.

Okay. So far so good, he thought as he turned to see what the wolves were doing.

He watched as one moved to his right and one to his left. Without thinking, he moved deeper into the woods. He'd gone about fifty feet into the brush when he realized he'd lost track of them. He froze, trying to listen for their movements.

Shit! Where did they go?

As if to answer him, he heard a growl to his left.

Damn!

He moved away from the growl, stumbling through the snow and tree branches

After ten minutes he stopped and listened. It was deadly silent, as only January in Northern Ontario can be. Even the breeze had stopped moving the tree branches.

Maybe I've lost them.

Then he heard a low growl on his right.

Damn it!

He moved to his left, continuing to struggle through the snow. But each time he stopped, each time he thought he'd lost them, he'd hear a growl. And each time it sounded closer.

He continued struggling, stopping every now and then to listen for the growl that always came, and continued to move away from it. At one of the stops he realized he couldn't feel his feet and that his hands felt completely frozen. Panic filled him.

I'm going to die out here, he thought fearfully, hearing the now familiar growl. But self-preservation took over, and breathing heavily, he trudged on.

After what seemed an indeterminable time, he halted, leaning against a tree. He breathing came in gasps and he was sweating. He couldn't remember when he'd opened his jacket, but he wasn't cold any longer. He felt completely exhausted, unable to move another foot. The exhaustion had vanquished the fear, and he stood calmly, looking back to see if he could spot the wolves.

I can't go on. If they want me, they can have me.

Growls came from both wolves, so close he thought he could touch them.

His instinct for survival reared again, and he rushed away from the growls.

After a few moments, he stopped, out of breath again.

This is it.

He looked around, trying to spot the wolves, but the darkness of the bush hid them.

Just then, a light a short distance away caught his eye.

He looked closer.

A house!

The wolves growled again, very close by.

He raced toward the light, out of the brush and into an open meadow, again struggling against the knee high snow.

"Help!" he yelled. "Help!"

As he got closer to the cabin, he saw the door open.

"Wolves!" he screamed. "There's wolves after me!"

The man who'd come through the door swung his flashlight past him, scanning the area, as he fell up the steps to the cabin.

"Thank God," he gasped.

"Where'd you come from?" the cabin owner asked as he helped him inside.

He slumped onto the nearest couch.

"I was coming down from Green Lake and went off the road."

"The Green Lake road?" the man exclaimed. "That's over five kilometers from here. How'd you find this cabin?"

"The wolves," he replied. "They were trailing me and I saw the lights."

"What wolves?" the man asked.

"They were right behind me. Didn't you see them?"

"There was nothing chasing you that I saw," the man replied.

"They were there," he said, slowly sitting up straight.

"Well, maybe. But there haven't been wolves in this area for decades."

"They were there. I saw them!" he yelled.

"Okay. Okay. I probably missed them. But you're safe now."

He relaxed again.

"Thanks."

"No problem," the man said as he got a cup of coffee for his visitor.

"I'm sorry," he said after he took the first sip. "I didn't mean to call you a liar."

The man chuckled.

"No offense taken. Flashlights don't show everything."

"Thanks."

"You know, I'm really tired," he said as he lay down on the couch.

The last thing he heard was the man saying "It's okay."

He awoke the next morning to the smell of fresh coffee. Looking around, he saw the cabin owner.

"Good morning," the owner said.

"Morning," he replied, slowly recalling the previous evening.

The man handed him a fresh cup of coffee.

"There really weren't any wolves," the man said.

He stood up.

"There were! They were not more than five feet from me when you came out!"

"No, there weren't any," he said firmly.

"Look outside!"

"I did. There's only your tracks."

He raced to the door, opened it and looked out.

He saw his tracks in the snow, and nothing else.

"You know," the cabin owner said, "I've been thinking. If you crashed where you said you did, with the temperatures the way they were last night, the only way you'd survive would have been to come here. And this isn't an easy place to find."

"I didn't know you were here."

"Well, I think someone upstairs did," he said smiling.

The man looked out the door again. There was no sign of any wolf tracks.

"Yea," he said softly, finally realizing what the wolves really were. "I guess someone did."

Tea and Conversation

By Susan A. Jennings

Everything about her seemed to deny her 95 years. She stood tall and straight with a healthy build. There was nothing wizened about Dorothy. She always wore a skirt or dress neatly pressed and stylish with an air of sophistication. Never did I see her wear slacks or gaudy floral prints. Not even her face had the deep wrinkles of such a long life and she was always smiling. She pinned her pure white hair on top of her head, not severe or harsh, but soft, as it flowed in waves up to a bun with the occasional wisp escaping, but never untidy.

To say I felt great affection for Dorothy would be a gross understatement; however, to say our love for each other was passionate would not fit either. Perhaps we were soul mates. When I looked into her soft, blue eyes, it was as if I could reach her soul and she, in turn, could touch mine.

Dorothy's delightful home was an 18th century English cottage. The heavy wooden beams and low ceilings made you instinctively duck as you walked through the doorway into a cozy lounge of comfortable chintz chairs and the lingering aroma of the morning baking.

"I have put the kettle on. I thought you might like a cup of tea?" she said, more as a statement rather than a question.

"That would be lovely," I replied.

The delicate china cups clinked as she placed the tea tray on the table. I marveled at her long, elegant fingers, her hands as steady as mine as she handed me the steaming tea.

"Cake?" she inquired

"Thank you," I replied taking a slice of fresh sponge cake, the result of the morning baking.

Conversation was easy with Dorothy. Her demeanor was always calm and gentle. I asked her what it was like to look back on so many years. She fell silent for a moment and then began to muse over all the changes she had observed, from one-room schools to laptop computers, penny stamps to email. I was mesmerized by her soft, gentle voice and fascinated by her memories as a young woman in the early 1900s. She compared the old and the new without the slightest hint of regret or yearning for the old days.

Sharing tea and conversation with Dorothy was surreal and, listening to her stories, was like being transported to another place and time, until reality returned, and it was time for me to leave.

We ambled down the path to the garden gate where she reluctantly slipped her arm out of mine and gently kissed me on the cheek. She stood, motionless, at the gate, surrounded by flowers. A wayward wisp of white hair moved gently in the breeze, her pale blue eyes smiling through to my soul as she waved goodbye. Her 95th year was to be her last. This was a perfect picture of Dorothy, and it will be etched in my memory forever.

Contributors

Anne Raina worked for many years in the public and not-for-profit sectors. She was a senior executive with a national disability organization when struck with a disabling autoimmune disorder herself.

She has been writing poetry, skits and short stories for friends and family since she was a child and she has two children's books in the works. Although previously published in magazines and newspapers, she has just published her first book. *Clara's Rib*, a true story, was co-authored with her sister Clara.

Her daughter, Kelly Anne McGahey, her son, Mark McGahey, and her step-son, Stefan Cameron work and live in Ottawa, Ontario. Anne lives with her husband, Grant Cameron, in Ottawa.

www.annerania.ca
www.clarasrib.ca

anneraina@rogers.com

Kathi Nidd grew up in Ottawa where she began weaving stories as soon as she could write. She continues to do so for pleasure and as a creative outlet. Kathi is a healthcare consultant and her travels to hospitals across North America provide great inspiration for her stories and characters. A strong love of nature and animals and an interest in the paranormal provide common themes in most of her works. She is currently devoted to completing her first novel.

Kathi resides in Barrhaven with her husband of 24 years and their 2 year old schnauzer.

Kathi.nidd@sympatico.ca

Rita Myres MSW, RSW. Rita grew up and began her working life in England, where she followed the path of science into research. After coming to Canada in 1970, initially for a one-year working adventure, she and her husband, Tony, discovered the great joy and challenge of raising three beautiful children. Between - times, Rita was a birth coach and lactation counselor for other Moms. Now a Canadian citizen and a clinical social worker, she continues to extend compassion beyond her family to her counseling clients. She writes to capture family memories for her children, her grandchildren and for Tony, her companion of 43 years.

r_myres@rogers.com

Susan Jennings RMT, IARP. After spending many years as an account executive for Lipton Food Service, Susan decided that instead of retiring she would pursue her three passions- writing, teaching and Reiki. First she published a book *'Save Some for Me'* her very personal story of marital abuse and subsequently raising five children alone. Her love of writing led her to develop a writing business *Just for Writers* coaching aspiring writers. Susan writes short stories and is working on a second book. She is also a Registered Reiki Professional and a practicing Reiki Master/Teacher.

Susan lives in Ottawa with her constant companion, Buddy.

www.justforwriters.ca
www.reiki-life-energy.com

sajennings@sympatico.ca

Tony Myres was born in England in 1944. He gained graduate and post-graduate degrees in chemistry before coming to Canada in 1970. After a distinguished scientific career in public health he retired in 2004 and was named Health Canada's first Scientist Emeritus. After more than 40 years of writing cool, objective scientific prose Tony decided to try creative writing, exploring memories and feelings associated with his early life in England, his family of origin, his schooldays and his later family life in Canada. Married in 1967 to Rita, they have three adult children and four grandchildren.

tmyres2004@yahoo.ca

Chantal Frobel, along with her mother and sister, grew up in the beautiful forests of Quebec. In her early teens, the family moved to the capital city Ottawa Ontario. By her early twenties, she purchased a new computer and started to research her family tree and discovered a relative named Friedrich Frobel, born 1782-1852, in Oberweissbach, a village in the Thuringian forest Germany, the inventor of kindergarten. She is now dedicated to her first children's fantasy novel in honor of Friedrich Frobel. Her favorite quote by Friedrich, "Nothing comes without a struggle". Chantal Frobel currently lives in Ottawa with her three furry friends.

Kit Flynn. Kit's writings originate from a long line of life experiences, handled with humour, insight and courage. She has a Business Administration degree from the University of Regina, a Canadian Securities Commission Certification, and a Certification in Conflict Resolution from St Paul's University. She most recently, established Kit Flynn & Associates, providing Health and Fitness for 50 plus. Kit is often asked to deliver motivational speeches and is personally committed to living each day with a positive, life-affirming attitude. She has two adult children, Jackson and Mackenzie, and lives with her spouse, Norm St-Georges, in Ottawa, Canada.

www.kitflynn.ca

Barry Alder grew up in Ottawa and has spent his career in the I.T. industry, where he authored a large number of technical documents. A long time science fiction fan and spiritual follower, he has written a number of short stories, and has the first three books of a four book spiritual science fiction series published. For more information on Barry and the series, please visit his web site at:

www.innervoices-novels.com